These are the last days of the Library of Doom.

The forces of villainy are freeing the Library's most dangerous books. Only one thing can stop Evil from penning history's final chapter – the League of Librarians, a mysterious collection of heroes who only appear when the Library faces its greatest threat.

Good books can send a shiver down a reader's spine.

TABLE OF CONTENTS

Chapter 1
REAR WINDOW....................................7

Chapter 2
SPINE STEALER............................15

Chapter 3
GETTING BACK.............................25

Chapter 1

REAR WINDOW

Thick snow **falls** between two tall buildings.

A long narrow alley squeezes between them.

A boy walks quickly down the alley.

His shoulders scrape against the wet walls.

At the end of the alley a tiny shop squats in an open space.

Snow falls on the sign hanging above its door.

The Dark Angel.

The
Dark
Angel

Books Old & Ancient
H. Pryce, Owner

The boy runs up to the door and pounds.

"Mr Pryce!" shouts the boy. "It's Vincent. I have your new book. Open up! It's cold out here."

The door does not open.

CRASH!

The sound of **breaking** glass comes from behind the shop.

The boy rushes around the building to reach the rear window.

Snow **drifts** through a jagged opening in the glass.

Then Vincent sees glass lying in the snow.

The window was broken from the inside.

A moan pierces the **darkness**.

The boy puts his package down.

Then he carefully **climbs up** on the broken window's sill.

He sees a **dark shape** spread out across the floor of the shop.

It has Mr Pryce's eyes.

It has Mr Pryce's hair.

But it does not have the shape of a man.

Chapter 2

SPINE STEALER

Mr Pryce lies on the floor of his shop.

His body has no backbone. It spreads like a puddle.

"Vincent," says Mr Pryce.

The voice is half cough, **half gurgle**.

Next to the fleshy blob is an ancient book.

It has thick leather covers, but no spine.

Vincent stares at the shapeless thing on the floor.

He is frozen in **horror**.

Then he hears a thud in the darkness beyond
Mr Pryce.

He slowly walks inside.

He is careful not to step in the **puddle** that
was once Mr Pryce.

Vincent hears a second **thud**.

An enormous shadow stomps out of the darkness.

The shadow's spine is thick leather.

A dozen long legs click against the floor.

A high, papery tail **curves** out from behind the shadow.

The point of the tail drips ink.

It waves slowly back and forth, aiming at Vincent.

The boy **cries out** and steps back.

He falls on the floor, into the puddle of the **slimy** shopkeeper.

The Spine Tingler's tail drips more ink.

A blob of ink falls towards Vincent's face.

But the ink **blows** sideways.

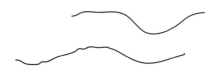

A strong **wind** comes in through the broken window.

Vincent looks up.

A young man steps over the sill into the crowded shop.

The wind blows harder.

The Spine Tingler shrieks in **anger**.

The wind tears at its spindly paper legs.

They rip off and fly backwards into the darkness.

Chapter 3

GETTING BACK

"Who … who are you?" asks Vincent.

"I'm a Librarian," the man says.

"Didn't you call for me?"

Vincent is **confused**.

The Librarian smiles.

"You left a new book in the back door. One that has never been read. That is always a signal to me that someone needs my help."

Suddenly, he **cries out**.

Hanging in the window, just outside, is a second monster.

It pulls its deadly tail from the neck of the Librarian.

The young man falls to the floor of the shop.

He groans in **pain**.

The thick collar of his jacket has been punctured.

"A book..." he gasps.

Vincent pulls a paperback from a nearby shelf.

"No!" the Librarian and Mr Pryce cry at the same time.

"I need a **hardback**," says the Librarian.
"Quickly!"

The second creature climbs through the window.

It reaches toward the kneeling man.

Its toothy mouth opens wide.

Vincent **tosses** a hardcover book to the Librarian.

The man holds the book above his head.

Its **spine grows** tall and sharp. Its edge gleams like a sword.

The book flies up and slices the evil creature in half.

Litres of black ink **burst** from the creature's gut.

Both the Librarian and the shopkeeper are drenched.

They disappear into the dark OOZE.

Flurries of snow blow in through the window.

The snow covers the black ink, turning the floor soft and white.

Slowly, two shapes **rise** up from the floor.

Snowmen.

"Mr Pryce!" cries Vincent.

The shopkeeper nods, exhausted. "Ah, back again," he says.

Before Vincent can reply, the snow is **sucked out** through the rear window.

The broken glass snaps back into place.

The shadow of a man flies past the window and into the dark sky beyond.

GLOSSARY

drenched – being completely wet

exhausted – feeling tired and worn out

fleshy – looking like skin, being soft and squishy

jagged – having sharp, uneven edges

moan – long, low sound that's made because of sadness or pain

puncture – make a hole with a sharp object

sill – piece of wood or stone at the bottom of a window or door

spindly – long and thin, often frail

spine – central, vertical part of a book's cover; the backbone of a person or animal

DISCUSSION QUESTIONS

1. The word "backbone" can sometimes mean courage or being firm. Who shows backbone in this story?

2. When Vincent goes to the back of the bookshop, he sees that someone has broken the window from the inside. Who do you think did it? Explain your answer.

3. At the end of the story, things suddenly return back to normal. Mr Pryce has a backbone again and the window is fixed. What do you think caused this to happen? Talk about some possible reasons.

WRITING PROMPTS

1. The Librarian seems to have special powers. Make a list of the powers you think he has in this adventure.

2. Where did the Spine Tinglers come from? Use the clues in the story and write a short paragraph explaining how they got into the shop.

3. The Librarian came to the shop because the new, unread book was a signal that someone needed help. Write a story about what would have happened if the Librarian had not come to the shop.

THE AUTHOR

Michael Dahl is the prolific author of the bestselling *Goodnight, Baseball* picture book and more than 200 other books for children and young adults. He has won the AEP Distinguished Achievement Award three times for his nonfiction, a Teachers' Choice Award from *Learning* magazine and a Seal of Excellence from the Creative Child Awards. He is also the author of the Hocus Pocus Hotel mysteries and the Dragonblood series. Dahl currently lives in Minneapolis, Minnesota, USA.

THE ILLUSTRATOR

Nelson Evergreen lives on the south coast of England with his partner and their imaginary cat. Evergreen is a comics artist, illustrator and general all-round doodler of whatever nonsense pops into his head. He contributes regularly to the UK underground comics scene, and is currently writing and illustrating a number of graphic novel and picture book hybrids for older children.